Baby Trauma & Bereavement Support

Making Miracles is a registered charity providing baby trauma
and bereavement support to families during and after a "high risk" pregnancy,
premature birth or baby loss.

Through this support and professional counselling we have seen many families suffering
from loss struggle to find the words to tell other children about what has happened.
This book is aimed to help alleviate that pressure and we have worked closely with the
author Joseph Hopkins to ensure it is positive, calm and helps in the bereavement journey.

It can even be said that "The Baby" could also be used with other family members and
friends. No one ever knows what to say when a baby dies and we hope this book will
help in the grieving process and perhaps comfort you to relieve some of the pain.

Learn more about Making Miracles at www.makingmiracles.org.uk and follow us on
Facebook "Making Miracles Charity"

Thank you for supporting the book - all profits will go direct back into the charity to
continue to support families through baby loss.

Kelly

Kelly Wells

Founder

A CIP catalogue record for this title is available from the British Library.

ISBN: 9781527219380   (paper back)

First Published (2017)

For every family
who have lost ...

The Baby

Written and illustrated by

Joseph Hopkins

in collaboration with

making miracles

Baby Trauma & Bereavement Support

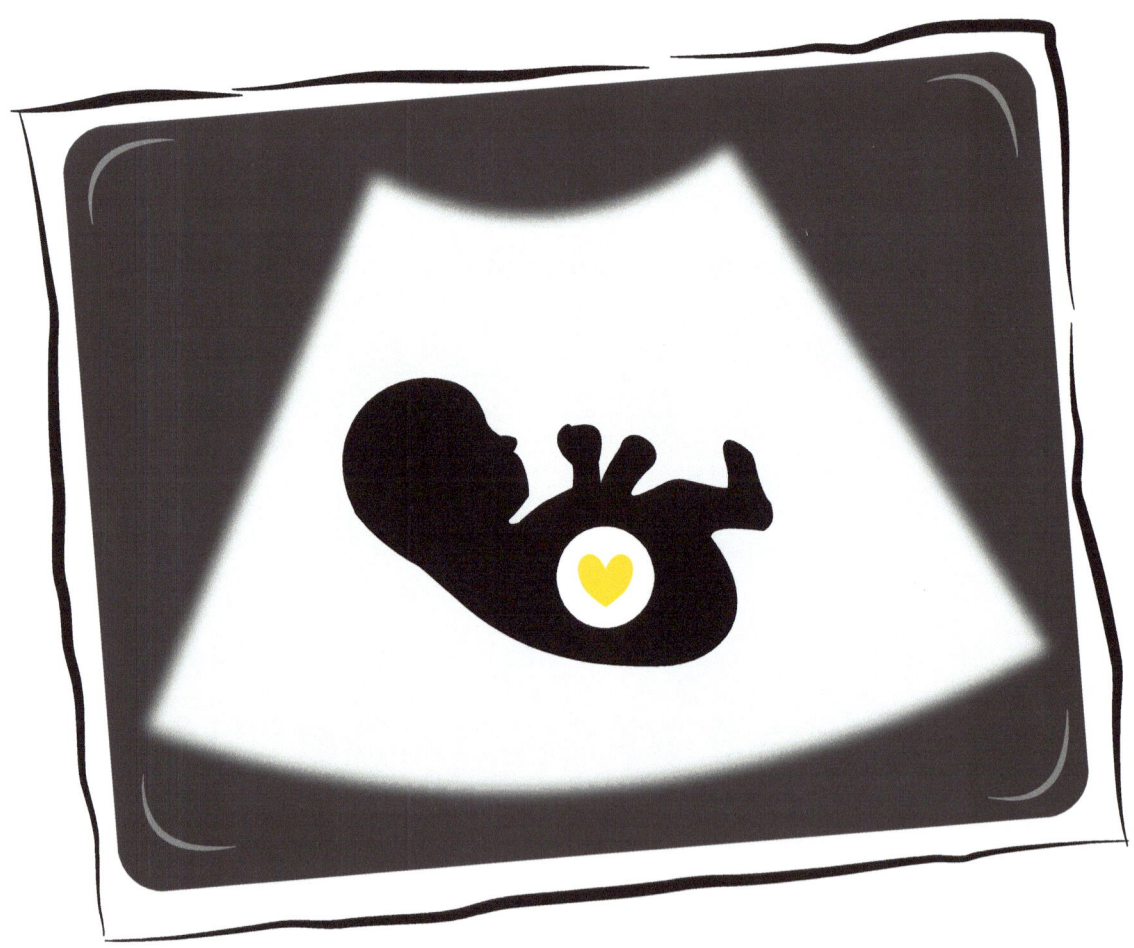

The baby is so special, innocent and sweet.

Loved by the family from their head to their feet.

There is a saying that's beautiful and describes baby,
whether they're a cute little boy, or a pretty little lady.

'Those we love don't go away...

forever in our hearts they're
here to stay.'

So though the baby leaving may feel painful or wrong,
try to stay calm and help each other stay strong.

Families should talk and discuss their pain.

Supporting one another helps the sun shine after rain.

It's fine to have sad days where there aren't any smiles,

but look to the sky and remember a while.

Think about baby and talk to the stars,

baby is part of you; both your heart and your scars.

Life is precious and with the baby that is true,

so live your life to the fullest like baby

would want you to.

Joseph Hopkins is an author illustrator from the U.K.

He has his own published titles and has also been the illustrator for other authors books.

Please visit Joseph's website to find out more.

www.josephhopkins.co.uk

Joseph is incredibly proud to of had the chance to collaborate with the Making Miracles charity for the production of this book.

Joseph would like to dedicate his work in this book to Charlie and his siblings Grace, Faith and Arthur.

The services that will continue through the funding of "The Baby"

Baby Memorial Garden:

Making Miracles has a Baby Memorial Garden which is open to parents who wish to visit a quiet, beautiful place to remember their lost baby. Welcoming to all parents and families no matter the gestation baby was, the reasons or cause or the time since this loss occurred. There is a House of Remembrance where parents and family can visit a Book of Remembrance. There is also a star which displays beautiful personalised slates and pebbles with a baby's date of birth or death engraved and a name if known. The garden is child friendly with a sibling's play area and fairy trail. Tranquil, beautiful and calm - a place for the whole family to come and remember.

Bereavement Counselling:

Families are offered free trauma and bereavement counselling with a professional counsellor. A one to one time to speak about emotions and feelings in a safe and secure environment. The feedback for this service has been outstanding and the Charity hope to be able to expand and continue it in order to help and reach more families needing that extra support.